D0465651

THE
LITTLE
LEFTOVER
WITCH

THE
LITTLE
LEFTOVER
WITCH

Florence Laughlin

SIMON & SCHUSTER
BOOKS FOR YOUNG READERS
New York   London   Toronto   Sydney   New Delhi

If you purchased this book without a cover, you should be aware that this book is stolen property. It was reported as "unsold and destroyed" to the publisher, and neither the author nor the publisher has received any payment for this "stripped book."

SIMON & SCHUSTER BOOKS FOR YOUNG READERS
An imprint of Simon & Schuster Children's Publishing Division
1230 Avenue of the Americas, New York, New York 10020

This book is a work of fiction. Any references to historical events, real people, or real places are used fictitiously. Other names, characters, places, and events are products of the author's imagination, and any resemblance to actual events or places or persons, living or dead, is entirely coincidental.
Text copyright © 1960 by Florence Laughlin
Text copyright renewed © 1988 by Florence Laughlin
Cover illustration copyright © 2013 by Kelly Murphy
All rights reserved, including the right of reproduction
in whole or in part in any form.

SIMON & SCHUSTER BOOKS FOR YOUNG READERS
is a trademark of Simon & Schuster, Inc.
For information about special discounts for bulk purchases,
please contact Simon & Schuster Special Sales at 1-866-506-1949
or business@simonandschuster.com.
The Simon & Schuster Speakers Bureau can bring authors to your live event.
For more information or to book an event, contact the
Simon & Schuster Speakers Bureau at 1-866-248-3049 or visit our website at
www.simonspeakers.com.
Also available in a Simon & Schuster Books for Young Readers
hardcover edition
Design by Laurent Linn
The text for this book is set in Minister Std.
Manufactured in the United States of America
0713 OFF
This Simon & Schuster Books for Young Readers paperback edition
August 2013
2 4 6 8 10 9 7 5 3 1
Library of Congress Cataloging-in-Publication Data
Laughlin, Florence.
The little leftover witch / Florence Laughlin. — 1st pbk. ed.
p. cm.
Summary: Stranded for a year on the ground, after a crash landing from her broom, a little witch is taken in by the Doon family, a situation which causes compromises on both sides, many happy times, and ultimately a big change for the little witch.
ISBN 978-1-4424-8677-5 (hardcover) — ISBN 978-1-4424-8672-0 (pbk.) —
ISBN 978-1-4424-8678-2 (eBook)
[1. Witches—Fiction. 2. Foster home care—Fiction. 3. Family life—Fiction.]
I. Title.
PZ7.L3703Li 2013
[Fic]—dc23
2012040276

For Caroline, Maureen, and Maggie

THE
LITTLE
LEFTOVER
WITCH

CONTENTS

1 The Broken Broom.................................1

2 The Witch Takes a Bath 6

3 How to Trick a Witch............................13

4 Felina Goes to the Store 18

5 A Permit to Keep a Witch.....................25

6 Felina Learns to Read 31

7 Grandfather Gives Felina a Gift 38

8 Christmas Is Coming!...........................46

9 A Visit to Dr. Perriwinkle 53

10 In a Witch's Sock 57

11 The Snow Witch...................................63

12 Halloween and Happy Birthday 69

1

The Broken Broom

It was Halloween.

The wind moaned like a thousand ghosts at the windows of the houses on Mockingbird Lane. Black cats chased one another across rooftops. And ghosts and goblins of all sizes ran through the streets.

Lucinda Doon was dressed like a ghost. A white sheet covered her clothes. It covered her yellow-gold hair and small brown shoes. It hid everything about her, except two laughing blue eyes, which peered out of two round holes.

She said, *"Boooooo,"* at Mr. Doon, her father. She said, *"Boooooo,"* at Itchabody, her great black cat. She went all around the block and frightened all the neighbors.

"Time to go upstairs to bed now," said Mrs. Doon, when Lucinda came back into her own house. "Halloween is over."

So Lucinda took off her ghost costume and hung it on the clothes tree. She washed her face and hands and put on her warm pajamas and crawled into bed. Then her mother kissed her tenderly and turned out the light.

Just as Lucinda was about to close her eyes she glanced out of the window—and thought she saw a witch! A black-clad witch, riding her broom across a pumpkin-yellow moon.

The little girl shivered happily and snuggled down under the covers to dream of the excitement she had had that night.

But Halloween wasn't over. Not quite.

In the middle of the night Lucinda woke up with a start. She heard a strange noise outside the window. It sounded like somebody crying. Or perhaps like somebody trying *not* to cry.

It was pitch-dark now. But Lucinda got out of bed and turned on the light and opened the window.

There, on the branch of the big bare mulberry tree, sat a bedraggled little witch! She wore a peaked hat. She had big staring eyes. And something like a raindrop ran down her face and fell off the tip of her pointed nose.

"Who are *you*?" cried Lucinda.

"I'm a witch, as you should plainly see," said the little witch crossly.

"Why are you crying?"

"I'm not crying." The little witch rubbed her eyes with the back of her fist. "I broke my broom and fell from the sky," she said. "And the sky was wet."

"How are you going to get home?" asked Lucinda anxiously.

"If I knew that, I wouldn't be sitting in this tree," snapped the strange little creature. "But I do know one thing—if I don't get back up there before the sun rises, I'll have to stay on the ground for a whole year. Till next Halloween."

Lucinda was almost sure she saw another tear. But she was too kind to mention it. She said, "Maybe I can help you. Mother has a brand-new broom. If you will come inside you may test it and see if it will fly."

The big branch was very near the window. Lucinda held out her arms and helped the little witch crawl inside the room.

Itchabody the cat came out from under the bed. He arched his back and his fur stood up like pins when he saw the visitor. "Meeeow!" he said whiningly.

"I pull cats' tails," said the little witch.

Itchabody backed away, hissing. But as Lucinda and the witch crept down the stairs to the broom closet, the cat scampered past them. When they got to the kitchen he rubbed his back against the visitor's long black robes and began to purr.

Lucinda took out her mother's brand-new broom. The little witch got astride it and jumped up and down. But the broom refused to fly.

Then she said:

"Abracadabra
Thirteen cats:
Sesame, sesame
Pickled Bats!"

But still the broom made no move to lift her from the floor. "It isn't magic," said the little witch ungraciously. "I knew it wouldn't work."

"Let's try the dust mop," suggested Lucinda helpfully.

So they tried the dust mop. They tried the sponge mop. They even tried Mrs. Doon's electric vacuum cleaner. And the little witch chanted all the magic words she knew, but she simply could not fly.

"That's too bad," said Lucinda. She felt very sorry for the little witch, in spite of her bad manners.

The little witch was worried, too. "I don't want to stay around here a whole year," she said. "I can't stand people!"

"Well, I'm afraid you'll have to stay, at least for tonight," replied Lucinda. "It's too cold to go outside again. You may sleep in my bed, and in the morning my father will think of a way to get you back home."

Lucinda and the little witch climbed back upstairs, but the little witch flatly refused to share Lucinda's bed.

"I don't like beds," she said. "I like dark places. I'll sleep in the closet."

So, while Lucinda crawled back into her warm, cozy bed, the weird little figure in the pointed hat slipped into the closet and closed the door.

Itchabody the cat joined her there.

2

The Witch Takes a Bath

When Lucinda opened her eyes once more the sun was shining. She felt very sure that she had just had a curious dream and that the little witch wasn't real at all.

But when she opened the closet door, there she was, sitting in a corner. Old Itchabody the cat jumped down from the witch's lap.

"Good morning," said Lucinda pleasantly.

The little witch glared at her. "What's good about it?" she demanded. But she got up and came out into the room, blinking her eyes.

"Do you have a name?" asked Lucinda.

"Of course I do. It's Felina. From 'feline,' you know. It means 'little cat,'" she said proudly. "The old witch who mixes potions named me that because I have green eyes."

"So you have!" cried Lucinda.

For the first time she noticed how enormous the little witch's eyes were, and how green. They looked very odd in her small pointed face. She did look like a kitten, too, thought Lucinda. Not pretty, of course. But then, one didn't expect a witch to be pretty.

"Come on," said Lucinda. "It's time to go down and eat breakfast. I'm as hungry as the three bears."

She put on her robe and slippers and went down to the kitchen, the little witch following close at her heels.

"Well, well," said Mrs. Doon, who was busy preparing breakfast, "what have we here?"

Mrs. Doon was seldom ever astonished at anything. But she did look a little surprised to find a witch in her kitchen.

"I want you to meet Felina, Mother," said Lucinda formally. "She's a witch. She's left over from Halloween. Felina broke her magic broom and can't fly back home, and I want Daddy to help her."

"Help her what?" asked Mr. Doon, coming in just then. He was tying his tie.

Then he looked down at Felina and all he could say was, "Well, well, well," and "WELL."

So Lucinda explained all about the broken broom and how Felina had spent the night in the closet. And how she didn't like people at all.

"So you see, Daddy," she added, "if we can find the broken broom, maybe you could mend it and—"

"Won't do any good," said the little witch impatiently. "The wind grabbed the broom and blew it far away. Witches can only fly on Halloween anyway."

"Well, well," said Mr. Doon again. He was concentrating on the problem. "Perhaps we could hire a helicopter to fly you home."

Felina stuck out her sharp little chin.

"You'd never find the way without a magic broom," she said. "I just have to stay down here till next Halloween. Then, if I'm out at midnight, I can catch onto another witch's broom and ride away."

Mrs. Doon was setting the table with bacon and eggs and pieces of golden-brown toast. She filled two big glasses with milk.

"Breakfast is ready, children," she said. "Come now and eat."

Lucinda was very hungry. She pulled up her chair and sat down. But Felina just sniffed.

"I only eat black-bat soup and jibbers' gizzards," she told them loftily.

"Well, we never have black-bat soup for breakfast," said Mrs. Doon firmly. She sat down and began to pour the coffee.

"And I'm not about to go out into the woods to shoot any jibbers," remarked Mr. Doon, taking his chair.

While Lucinda and her parents ate every bite of their breakfast, the little witch just sat in a corner and glowered at them.

"What are we going to do about her?" asked Mr. Doon in a low voice.

"I don't know," said Mrs. Doon. "She is obviously lost, poor little thing. And I must say, she does have a dreadful disposition."

"Oh, please, Mother," whispered Lucinda, "let her stay with us. I don't think she is really mean. I think she's just afraid of things." She thought it would be great fun to have a real witch to play with.

"We do have enough room," said Mrs. Doon slowly. "I suppose she could stay here till somebody claims her."

So it was decided.

"I'm going to the office now," said Mr. Doon, "but I'll report the matter to the police. And I'll ask around town to see if anyone is missing a little witch. We'll see about it tonight."

He got up and kissed his wife good-bye. He kissed Lucinda good-bye. He thought of kissing Felina. But when he looked in her direction she made a wicked face at him, so off he went.

"First thing we'd better do," said Mrs. Doon, after she had done the dishes, "is to comb Felina's hair and give her a bath."

"Witches never comb their hair," said Felina. "And they never take baths. Never, never, NEVER."

"Witches who stay in my house do," said Mrs. Doon. "Run and fetch a nice clean comb, Lucinda."

Lucinda brought a comb and brush. Mrs. Doon put the kitchen stool on the back porch and perched Felina upon it. Quickly, she grabbed off the funny little cone-shaped hat and hung it on a nail.

"My hat, my hat," screamed Felina. "Give me back my hat."

"Just as soon as you get your hair combed," said Mrs. Doon quietly.

So the little witch was forced to have her hair combed. It was so tangled that it took all morning long to get the snarls out.

Mrs. Doon combed on one side and Lucinda brushed on the other. They combed and they brushed and they brushed and they combed. And the little witch set up an awful fuss.

She screeched and she yelled. But Lucinda and Mrs. Doon were just as careful and gentle as they could be.

"Save the snarls," insisted the little witch. "Witches' snarls are full of magic."

But Mrs. Doon just dumped them in the trash. And they combed and brushed and brushed some more, until the little witch's hair was as smooth and shiny as a cap of black satin and curled up at the ends just like Lucinda's.

"I hate it!" declared Felina. And just to be wicked, she stirred it into a mess again.

Mrs. Doon patiently combed it once more and

made two silky braids. She tied the ends tightly with red ribbons.

But when Mrs. Doon forgot and started to take the dreary little hat out to the trash, Felina jumped from the stool.

"Don't throw away my hat," she pleaded. "Witches wear their hats always."

The poor little witch looked so alarmed that Mrs. Doon came back quickly. She put the peaked hat on Felina's freshly combed hair and the little creature reached up and held tightly on to it, afraid it might be whisked away again.

"I keep my magic in my hat," she said.

"Now, then," said Mrs. Doon with a sigh, "we must wash your dress. It's all rumpled and muddy. You go with Lucinda and take a nice bath, and then you may put on some of her clean clothes."

"I won't," said the little witch.

"Oh, come, take a bath," pleaded Lucinda. "It's lots of fun. I have soap that floats and a boat that sails."

"I want my own dress," said Felina.

"Very well," said Mrs. Doon. "I'll wash your little black dress and you may put it back on."

And that is what happened. Lucinda and Felina got into a tub of warm, sparkling water and splashed about. Felina wore her hat and refused to wash behind her ears and she dashed soapsuds all over Itchabody, who was passing by. She gave a little cackling laugh when he went, *"Phttt,"* and hid under the washbasin.

But Felina did come out quite clean. And Mrs. Doon wrapped her in a big towel and let her sit on a stool and watch her dress go around and around in the automatic washer. Then she starched it and ironed it and Felina put it back on.

That afternoon, Lucinda saw the little witch standing before the mirror, turning from side to side. Her clothes were clean, her hair was smooth, and her face was clean.

"You look very nice," said Lucinda kindly.

The little witch whirled about. "Bats and cats!" she said in a sassy voice.

Then she flew up the stairs and went into the closet and closed the door. She refused to come out to play, and she refused to come out for lunch. She didn't come downstairs again until she heard Mr. Doon's car drive into the garage that evening.

3

How to Trick a Witch

Mr. Doon was amazed when he came in and saw Felina sitting on the steps, holding the cat.

"Why, she looks almost like a human being, Mary," he said to his wife. "Her hair is beautiful, though she still looks a little spooky in that awful hat. I don't suppose there is anything we can do about her pointed nose and chin."

"There's something *I* can do," said Mrs. Doon. "I'm quite sure black-bat soup and jibbers' gizzards aren't very nourishing, even for witches. She has refused to eat all day, so I fixed an extra-special supper. The poor little thing seems half starved."

So Mrs. Doon and Lucinda set the table together. They put on a big platter of steaming chicken and dumplings. They brought in vegetables and salad and ice-cold milk. For dessert there was peach cobbler and ice cream!

"Come, little witch," Mrs. Doon called then, "and eat your supper."

But the little witch refused to come. "You can't make me eat," she said, stamping her foot and glaring at the good food.

"Nobody is going to make you," said Mrs. Doon with a smile.

Felina crawled under the dining room table. The family sat down to eat.

First Mr. Doon said the blessing. Then he served the chicken and dumplings and vegetables.

"Mmmmmmm! This is the best chicken I ever tasted," said Lucinda.

"The dumplings and gravy are delicious," said Mr. Doon.

"The finest baked squash I ever tasted," said Lucinda's mother, "if I did bake it myself."

For a while nothing was heard but the sound of forks scooping up the food. The smell of the delicious things to eat drifted over the edge of the table and made the little witch's nose twitch.

Then Mr. Doon reached into the dumpling platter and brought up a gizzard. "I do believe that looks like a jibber's gizzard, Mary," he said.

"It certainly does."

And all at once a spooky little black hat appeared above the edge of the table. The little witch edged slowly toward the empty chair and slipped into it.

In a twinkling Mr. Doon dropped the savory gizzard

onto Felina's plate. He heaped chicken and dumplings beside it. Mrs. Doon quietly pushed the glass of milk within reach of a small hand.

Not a word more was said. But the food disappeared like magic. The glass was refilled with milk. Halfway through a big dish of ice cream and cobbler, the spoon dropped from the hand and the little peaked hat began to bend toward the table.

Mr. Doon left his chair and picked up the drowsy little witch and carried her to Lucinda's room. Mrs. Doon and Lucinda tiptoed after them.

Carefully, carefully, they removed her shoes and unhooked her black dress. But the instant they touched the peaked black hat Felina came awake in a flash. She jumped off Mrs. Doon's lap.

"You fell asleep," said Mrs. Doon gently. "We were going to put you into Lucinda's nice, warm bed."

"No, no, *no*," cried Felina. "Witches never sleep in beds like that."

"You may wear some of my fuzzy pajamas," said Lucinda. She ran to get a pair from her bureau.

Felina pushed them aside. She stood in the middle of the floor, glaring at them all.

Then Mr. Doon had to take over.

He looked down at the defiant little figure. "You are going to put on those pajamas and get into that bed, Felina," he said sternly, "or I will spank you."

Felina put her hands behind her. "You can't spank witches," she declared. She seemed about to cry.

"I don't want to spank a witch," said Mr. Doon kindly, "but I will if I have to." He sat down on the bed. "Felina, come here. I want to tell you something."

Slowly, she obeyed him.

"There are a few things that grown-ups know more about than children do. While you live in our house we want you to be happy. You may have your own way about all the little things, like what kind of ice cream you'll eat and what toys you'll play with. But when something is really important you must obey.

"When Lucinda's mother or I say to you, 'that's an order,' you do it," said Mr. Doon.

"But why can't I sleep in the closet?"

"Because the floor is cold and drafty. You might get sick, and we would feel very sad about it."

"Would you?" She stared at him from her sharp green eyes.

"We certainly would," said Mr. Doon. "Now get into those pajamas and crawl into bed. *And that's an order.*"

"All right," agreed Felina. "But I won't take off my hat!"

Mr. Doon laughed. "That's your business," he said.

Refusing any help, Felina put on the pajamas and got into bed with Lucinda.

Later, when Mr. Doon came in to check the covers, he smiled. On one pillow lay the golden head of his daughter. On the other, her hat askew, the dark head of Felina. Beside her, curled up in a black ball on the coverlet, was Itchabody.

4

Felina Goes to the Store

Mr. Doon worked for the local newspaper. The next day, when he went down to the office, he put this ad in the paper.

FOUND
One very small witch with green
eyes and black hair. Anyone
interested contact George Doon
on Mockingbird Lane.

He had already reported the matter to the police and they asked him to bring Felina in to the station for investigation. So Felina went with Mr. Doon in his peacock-blue sports car. She wanted to take Itchabody along, but Mr. Doon got his "grown-up" expression ready, so Felina agreed to leave the cat at home.

The police asked her a lot of questions, which she refused to answer. They took her fingerprints and her picture. They took a front view of her scowling little face and a side view of her profile. But every time the photographer snapped the camera she moved her head.

They had to take seventeen shots and waste a lot of county film before they could get a likeness.

"I'll bet no one will claim this one," muttered the sergeant as he typed out the bulletin.

It wasn't until after Felina had gone that he discovered the mysterious fingerprints on all the important papers on his desk. He spent the whole afternoon using ink remover. "Little demon," said the sergeant.

There were no replies to Mr. Doon's ad. And no replies to the All-Points-Bulletin that the police circulated. There were rumors in town about a traveling band of gypsies having gone through. There were stories about a mysterious airplane accident in the hills and about a family being lost in a landslide.

But nobody came forth to claim Felina. Either nobody had lost a witch that Halloween, or if anybody had, they didn't want her back again.

So Felina went on living with the Doon family. Lucinda was very happy about the whole thing. She thought it was wonderful to have a playmate. Even a witch who was sometimes cross.

Lucinda liked to play house and she was always asking Felina to play with her.

"You may have Betsey for your little girl," she told the little witch one day. She took Betsey down from the shelf. Betsey was her second-best doll, somewhat old and battered but still very useful.

Felina eyed Lucille, whom Lucinda was cuddling. Lucille was as gorgeous as a princess, with tiny high-heeled slippers on dainty plastic feet. Felina swept Betsey into a corner.

"I don't like dolls," she declared. "They're too silly. I like bats and cats. I'll have Itchabody for my baby."

So Felina began to pretend that Itchabody was her doll. She asked Mrs. Doon for a scrap of black cloth and made a tiny witch's hat for him. She tied it under his chin and to the back of his collar, so he couldn't scratch it off.

Naturally, Itchy wasn't very much pleased at first. But Felina was a clever little witch. She asked Mrs. Doon to loan her a leftover sardine. She fed the cat a nibble at a time and said some magic words.

In a twinkling old Itchabody was sound asleep in the doll buggy, under a blanket.

Felina played happily with Lucinda that morning. She even took the cat along when they walked to the supermarket with Lucinda's mother. Of course Mrs. Doon didn't know about it. Not until they passed by the frozen meat bin, that is.

Itchabody must have got a whiff of something good, because he suddenly leaped out of the doll buggy and landed slam in the middle of the smoked herring tray!

It looked delicious and it must have smelled delicious. But it was hard to get at because it was frozen solid. So Itchabody kept scratching and digging and licking, trying to loosen a fish.

And Felina stood by, waiting patiently for him to get through, while Lucinda and Mrs. Doon went on.

Felina reached over and helped a little. And finally the two of them got a lovely herring free. But meanwhile, something tragic had happened.

The end of Itchabody's tail had got into some spilled liquid and had frozen fast to the freezer. When he grabbed up his fish and tried to run off with it, he discovered that he was a prisoner.

Now, the cat had always been treated with kindness. He couldn't understand what had happened. So he gave a horrible yowl and jumped in the air.

But he was held fast. So he screeched again.

"Mother, Mother," screamed Lucinda, running back, "Itchabody's getting frozen up."

"Itchy, Itchy," cried the little witch, "come to Felina."

At the sound of her voice the cat howled again. And Felina scrambled up into the freezer bin to his rescue.

Now all the customers in the store came running. The manager came running.

The manager tried to grab poor Itchabody. But the cat hissed and scratched. He tried to grab Felina, but she hissed too.

Then Mother came running from the soap

department. When she saw what was happening, her face got all red.

"Get out of there, Felina," she cried.

Then a big man who was eating a triple-deck cherry cone began to laugh. He laughed so hard he choked on a cherry and began to splutter. His wife had to stop watching the excitement and pound him on the back.

"Get that cat out of my freezer," cried the manager. "Get that kid out of there."

"That's not a kid," said Lucinda helpfully. "That's a real live witch. She belongs to us."

By now Felina was sitting on a frozen turkey with the cat in her lap—the part that wasn't stuck, that is. She was crooning a little witch's song, trying to console Itchabody, whose tail was slowly freezing.

"Turn off the machines and let him defrost," suggested one of the customers.

"Use your witch magic, Felina," said Lucinda.

"That's a good idea," said Felina. And in a loud shrill voice she said:

"Abracadabra
Thirteen bats:
Sesame, sesame
Frozen cats!"

Then she bent down and breathed on Itchabody's tail and pulled very gently.

Suddenly the black cat sprang free. He grabbed his smoked herring, bounded out of the freezer, and ran to hide behind a bin of onions.

"Get that kid out of there before *she* gets stuck," shouted the manager. He probably would have torn his hair, except he didn't have any.

Then poor Mrs. Doon lifted Felina out of the meat bin. Lucinda ran to catch Itchabody and knocked over a great pile of canned tomatoes.

Mrs. Doon's face was redder than ever when she finally gathered them all together. Cat, witch, girl, and all—she shoooooed them out of the market.

"I forgot my doll buggy," wailed Lucinda.

"I'll get it," said Mrs. Doon. She was so angry she could hardly speak. "But don't you ever—don't you *ever* bring that cat to the store again," she said to Lucinda and Felina.

"If you do," she added, "I'll—I'll *spank* you both till you can't sit down."

It wasn't at all like Mrs. Doon to become so angry. But she was only human.

Itchabody just looked up at her and whined. He wasn't very happy, because he had lost his herring.

Lucinda and Felina were very quiet. Mrs. Doon

went back into the store to settle her bill for groceries and pay for the damages.

By that time the manager had calmed down and was picking up cans of tomatoes, TWO FOR 25¢.

"Accidents will happen, Mrs. Doon," he said. But his manner was pretty chilly. And after that Mrs. Doon only traded at that supermarket on Wednesdays.

That was the manager's day to go to Kiwanis Club.

5

A Permit to Keep a Witch

The story about Itchabody and the herring went all around town. And as stories do, it grew and GREW. Some people swore that after Felina had left the grocery store, all the labels on the cans were turned upside down. Someone else said that all the pumpkins popped their seeds when Felina stared at them.

"It's bad luck to have a witch about," everybody said.

Mr. Doon heard all about it down at the newspaper office. When he came home that evening Lucinda was sitting in one corner of the living room. She had a tall dunce cap perched on her head.

Felina was sitting in another corner with her peaked black hat.

Mr. Doon looked down at them and began to laugh. He laughed and he laughed and he laughed until the tears ran down his cheeks.

"I hear you went shopping today, Mary," he said to Mrs. Doon.

And Mrs. Doon said, "It *wasn't* funny."

Then Mr. Doon looked down on the floor. And there was Itchabody in his little peaked hat, lying on the gray rug purring away. Mr. Doon began to laugh all over again.

Then he kissed Lucinda on the cheek, he chucked Felina under the chin, and he kissed his wife's pretty, cross face.

"Life must have been very dull," he said, "before this little witch came to live with us."

The strange thing is, when he said that, everyone began to laugh, even Mrs. Doon. They laughed and laughed and laughed.

Even the manager of the supermarket laughed a little himself, when he told his wife what had happened in the store that day.

The kindly Doon family found it slightly embarrassing now and then to have a witch in their midst. There was the matter of the hat, to begin with.

Felina insisted upon wearing it constantly, except when she had her hair shampooed, of course.

She wore it to bed. She wore it at the table. She even wore it to church on Sunday. And the Doons allowed her to because they realized how important it was to her.

"I keep my magic in it," Felina always said.

And strange things did seem to happen when Felina was around.

There was the day, for instance, when Mrs. Brown from next door arrived to say that all of her chrysanthemums had lost their heads.

"Every last one of them—beheaded, like that!" She snapped her fingers. "And I thought I saw that little houseguest of yours behind the gate," she added.

"Are you quite sure Clarence didn't do it?" asked Mr. Doon, over Mrs. Doon's shoulder.

Now, it was well known that Mrs. Brown did not like children very much. And it was little wonder because she had one of her own named Clarence. Clarence was what is sometimes known as a "problem child."

"Clarence has been home with a cold all day," said Mrs. Brown. "I want a complete investigation."

"You'll get it," said Mr. Doon politely. And he politely closed the door.

He asked Lucinda if she knew anything about the chrysanthemums. He asked Felina. She said, "What are chrisanteums?" He looked under the bed and behind the clothes in the closet and in the mulberry tree.

No chrysanthemums. It wasn't until weeks later when he filled his pipe from his humidor and took a big puff, that he began to suspect what might have happened to the flowers from Mrs. Brown's garden.

"Ugh," he said. But it was too late to explain to

Mrs. Brown because by that time she was planting amaryllis bulbs.

Then there was the time when Mrs. Doon went to make an apple pie. All of the apples had vanished from the refrigerator. Mr. Doon knew nothing about them. Lucinda knew nothing about them.

Felina just set her small pointed chin and shook her head. But that very day, when Mrs. Doon took off the witch's hat to shampoo the little creature's hair, seventeen apple cores fell on the bathroom floor!

Felina looked down at them, her eyes green and wide, as though she had never seen them before. And Mrs. Doon said nothing at all. She just began very gently to unbraid the black hair.

That evening, after supper, Mrs. Doon brought a big basket into the dining room and set it on the sideboard. Then she called all the family to come see it.

It was full of delicious red apples, big oranges, bananas, and tangerines.

Mrs. Doon said, "All the food in this house belongs to all the people in it. Whenever you want an apple or an orange, just help yourself."

When the fruit vanished, the basket was always filled again. That was Mrs. Doon's kind of magic.

When the days passed by and nobody came to claim the little witch, Mr. Doon decided it was time to do something legal about the matter. So the whole family got into the blue sports car and went down to the court-house to get a permit to keep a witch.

"A witch, eh?" said the old judge. He looked down at the thin little creature. "Looks more like a scarecrow to me."

Now, he didn't know witches had such good ears, or he wouldn't have spoken so loud.

Felina said defiantly, "Witches are supposed to be scary. And I'm a mean witch, so there."

"Ahem," said the judge. He put on his bifocal glasses and peered down at his papers. "You, George Doon, want a permit to keep a witch—for how long?"

"About a year," said Mr. Doon, "till next Halloween, that is." And he explained how Felina had broken her broom and would have to stay on the ground till next Halloween. And how she had no other place to live.

"Well, of course, we could put her in an institution," said the judge. "If you don't want the trouble, that is—"

"Oh, but we do want her," said Mrs. Doon.

"Please, sir, Mr. Judge," said Lucinda, who was standing beside Felina. "Let her live at our house."

"Very well then." The judge scribbled on the form in front of him. "Granted. Temporary permit to keep one small witch till next Halloween. That'll be one dollar."

"Thank you, your honor," said Mr. Doon.

He started to leave with his family.

"Just a minute," said the judge, pointing a finger at the little witch. "She'll have to go to school, you know. Even a witch needs an education."

6

Felina Learns to Read

"Don't want to go to school," said Felina emphatically when the family arrived home.

"Everyone must go to school sometime," said Mrs. Doon. "I went to school. Lucinda goes to school. And even a very small witch must get an education."

"I got an education," insisted Felina. "In Small Magic school. Next year when I go back, I'll go to Big Magic school. The old Wizard teaches that, and you learn to do big mischief."

"Well, down here," said Mr. Doon, "we don't go to school to learn mischief. We go to learn to read and write and to be good Americans. Tomorrow morning you will go to school with Lucinda."

"Won't," said the little witch. She glared at Lucinda's father out of defiant green eyes.

Mr. Doon glared back, looking very stern, which was hard for him to do because he was in the habit of smiling so much.

"I won't," repeated the little witch, "unless," she added in a very small voice, "unless that is an order."

"It's an order," said Mr. Doon. Then he smiled and knelt down so that he could look into her troubled little face. "Someday you'll be very glad you went to school, honey."

"All right," agreed Felina. But she didn't look too happy about it, and Lucinda put an arm around her.

"I'll help you with your lessons," said Lucinda.

"I'll get you some paper and pencils and some new school shoes," said Mrs. Doon. "You'll have to wear some of Lucinda's dresses for a while," she added. "I believe they'll just fit you."

The very next day Felina went off to school with Lucinda, still wearing her funny black hat. Mrs. Doon walked along to talk to the teacher.

"Please let Felina wear the hat in school," Mrs. Doon said. "It seems important to her. Before long I hope she will forget about it."

Miss Prang, the teacher, looked doubtfully at her strange new pupil. "Well, we'll try it," she said.

At first the children were fascinated at having a real live witch in their class. Lucinda told them all how Felina was left over from Halloween, and the children on the playground gathered around her, asking a hundred questions. Where did she live and how did it feel to ride on a broom. And could she really do magic tricks.

But all Felina would say was, "Cats and bats!" Or,

"Bats and cats!" And she stayed very close to Lucinda's side.

Everything went quite well for a time. Felina had a seat behind Lucinda and listened very quietly to the lessons. She enjoyed the crayon drawing and made an excellent picture. But all she wanted to draw was jack-o'-lanterns, bats, and cats.

"Before long it will be Thanksgiving time," suggested Miss Prang. "Why don't you make a turkey?"

Felina refused. But she did make a pumpkin in a corn field, and Miss Prang said it was the best in the class.

Then it came time for reading. Miss Prang went down Felina's row, asking every child to read from the book. Tommy read well, Lucinda read very nicely.

"Now, Felina," said Miss Prang. "Let's see how well you can read."

Felina stood up, holding the book in front of her. She looked at the pages with black letters and pictures. She opened her mouth, but she didn't read a word.

She stood there for a long time. Finally Miss Prang said, "You may sit down."

And all of the children giggled. All except Lucinda.

A boy in the back of the room, a boy with pumpkin-yellow hair and freckles, whispered, "Some magic!" The children laughed again and Miss Prang rapped on the desk.

After recess, when the children came back to class, Felina was not in her seat. They found her in the cloakroom, sitting on the floor among the overshoes.

"Come back to your seat, Felina," said Miss Prang quietly.

"Is—is that an order?" asked Felina.

Miss Prang looked surprised, but she said yes, very quickly. So Felina went forlornly back to her seat. All the children stared at her.

When the little witch came home that evening her hat looked very strange. As though it had a block of wood hidden in it, or maybe a book.

She refused to eat any supper and crept upstairs without saying a word to anyone.

When Mrs. Doon went to see what was the matter, she found Felina in the closet. She had Mr. Doon's flashlight, and her head was bent over the reader.

"What are you doing, darling?" asked Lucinda's mother.

"I'm learning to read," said Felina. "All the other children can read. Miss Prang says if I can't read I'll have to go back with the baby class."

The proud little chin was trembling.

Mrs. Doon sat right down on the floor and gathered the little witch up in her arms. "You are going to read," she said softly. "You're going to be the best reader in that old class.

"Come down and eat some supper now. After that, we will have a reading lesson."

That's how Felina came to learn to read.

Mrs. Doon helped. Mr. Doon helped. Lucinda helped. Every night, after school, they worked over the reader. Page by page. Word by word. Felina may have been a witch, but she was a smart one. In just a few days she was sounding out words and reading sentences.

One day, when Lucinda and Felina came running home from school, they found a stranger on the front porch. That is, he was a stranger to Felina. But not to Lucinda!

Lucinda opened the gate and gave a cry of delight. "Grandfather! Grandfather!" she shouted. And she rushed up the walk and jumped right into his arms.

Now, Grandfather Doon was a beautiful man. He looked like his son George only he was older. He was tall, and his hair was silver gray, and he had laughed so much all of his life that the laugh was part of his skin.

Felina stood at the gate all by herself and watched the wonderful scene.

Grandfather Doon said, "I came to spend the holidays, Lucinda. I flew in a great jet plane from New Haven. I flew over the rivers and over the mountains and—"

All at once he looked past Lucinda's golden head and saw Felina in her funny little hat. "What ho!" he said, setting Lucinda down. "Who have we here?"

"That's Felina, Grandfather. That is our little witch." Lucinda ran to Felina and led her to the porch. "She's our very own witch and she lives at our house. Oh, could you be *her* grandfather too?" asked Lucinda.

"Why of course!" declared Grandfather Doon. And suddenly he did a surprising thing. He reached down and picked Felina up in his arms. Books, witch hat, and all.

"Saints be praised!" he cried. "A real live witch! I've never been introduced to one before."

And he hugged her warmly and kissed her sharp little nose. Then he held his head back, looking at her, laughing till his blue eyes sparkled.

Felina started to laugh too. Not a little witch's cackle either, but a real laugh that sounded more like the lovely trill of a bird.

Mrs. Doon heard it and came running to the porch in her apron. Mr. Doon heard it as he drove down the lane and stepped on the gas.

"Grandfather, Grandfather Doon," cried Felina. *"I can read."* She told him the news she had been bursting to share. "Today in class I read a whole page. And nobody laughed."

"Well, wonder of wonders!" said Grandfather, as

though he had heard of a miracle. He put the little witch down on the porch. "I can't wait for a demonstration."

So right then and there, Felina showed them. They all sat down on the steps. Mrs. Doon, Mr. Doon, and Lucinda. Grandfather sat next to Felina and helped hold the book.

Felina read a whole page about Dick and Jane and Spot. They all agreed that it was wonderful. Even Itchabody came and listened politely.

7

Grandfather Gives Felina a Gift

After that Felina did very well in school. The other children accepted her as one of them, in spite of her strange little hat. She was so busy learning to read and to make her letters, she had little time to practice her Small Magic.

One day Suzie Parker, one of the pupils, brought a box of tiny pink envelopes to school. She gave one to Lucinda and one to Felina and one to every other child in the class.

They were invitations to a birthday party!

Felina had never been to a party, of course. But Lucinda was very excited.

"I'll wear my pink dress with ruffles, and you may wear my yellow dress with ruffles," she said to Felina.

They looked very pretty, walking down the block, all dressed up. Lucinda carried a present for Suzie in her hand. Felina carried her present in her black witch's hat.

The party was great fun at first. Felina played all the games. She ate candy and popcorn. She even laughed now and then.

Then Mrs. Parker brought in the birthday cake. It had white icing, decorated with pink roses. The candles flickered and danced as the children sang:

"Happy birthday to you!
Happy birthday to you!
Happy birthday, dear Suzie, . . ."

Everyone sang, except Felina, of course. She did not know the words.

Then the children began to chatter excitedly about birthdays.

"Mine is in May," shouted Lucinda. "I'm going to have Mayflowers on my cake."

"Mine is in July," cried Tommy Jones. "I'm going to have flags."

They all shouted and laughed and laughed and shouted. Except Felina.

Then Mrs. Parker set the wonderful cake in front of Suzie. Suzie took a deep breath and puffed out her cheeks.

Then—something very mysterious happened.

Before the little girl could say poof! and blow out the candles they went out all by themselves! One by one. Phft, phft, phft. Tiny curls of smoke rose from the wicks.

Suzie was so startled she began to cry.

Then all the colored balloons began to pop. One by one. Bang! Bang! Bang!

Then the most dreadful thing of all happened. The beautiful new birthday doll, which was perched on a table near Felina, came tumbling down. She fell—plunk—right into a big plate of ice cream. And alas! It was chocolate.

There was a great commotion, with everyone squealing at once. And when Lucinda looked around for the little witch, she wasn't to be found anywhere.

"It was the little witch who did it," said one of the children. "She cast a bad spell on Suzie's party."

"It wasn't, it wasn't," cried Lucinda. "Felina is not a bad witch anymore." Then she opened the door and ran as fast as she could down Mockingbird Lane.

Felina was hiding in the closet when Lucinda reached home. She wouldn't open the door until Grandfather Doon came upstairs and asked her to, very politely.

He led her down the stairs. And just as they reached the lower floor, the phone rang.

It was Mrs. Parker. She told Mrs. Doon all about what had happened at Suzie's party.

"The children believe that your little witch was up to some of her tricks," said Mrs. Parker. "My Suzie is crying right now because her new doll has chocolate ice cream in her hair."

"I'm very sorry," said Mrs. Doon. "I'll try to get to the bottom of it right away."

She turned to Felina, who was standing in the middle of the floor.

"Felina," she said gently, "did you perform some of your Small Magic at Suzie's party?"

"It was an awful old party," said the little witch.

"I want you to tell me the truth," said Mrs. Doon. "Whatever you say, Felina, I am going to believe you.

"Now I'll ask you once more. Did you play tricks at the party?"

For an awful moment the little witch said nothing. Then she turned and ran upstairs.

Lucinda started to follow her, but her mother held her back. "Let Felina think about this for a while," she said quietly. "I think she will come down when she is ready and tell us the truth."

Mrs. Doon was mending socks when Felina crept slowly down the stairs a half-hour later. Grandfather Doon and Lucinda were watching television.

The little witch stood in front of Mrs. Doon. Her head bowed. "I did it," she said. "I spoiled the party."

"But why?" asked Mrs. Doon gently. She put her arm around the little figure.

For a moment Felina was silent. Then she burst out, "They all have birthdays! Everyone in the world has a birthday but me."

"But you must have a birthday, dear," said Mrs. Doon. "Can't you remember when it is?"

Felina shook her head. "Witches don't have birthdays, I guess," she replied. "Witches just *are*."

Grandfather Doon switched off the television set and stood up.

"This is a disgraceful situation," he declared. "Everybody deserves to have a birthday. I'll tell you what, Felina, you may have *my* birthday."

"May I?" cried Felina. Her small face lighted up, then grew cloudy again. "But then, you wouldn't have any."

"Oh, my goodness," said Grandfather Doon, "I've had so many birthdays I've almost lost count. I've had dozens of cakes and blown out hundreds of candles. I don't need mine anymore. I'll be glad for you to enjoy it. October thirty-first, that's when it is."

"Why that's the same date as Halloween," said Lucinda.

"So it is, and very fitting, too," said Grandfather. "And just to make it legal," he added, "we'll put it in writing."

With those words, he sat down at the desk and drew a piece of paper toward him. In bold, black ink, he wrote these words:

For the sum of one hug and other valuable considerations, I, George P. Doon Sr.,

do hereby sell and bequeath to little Miss
Felina one birthday—happily used for sixty-
one years but still in good condition. Said
birthday is celebrated on October 31st of
each year and is to be hers from this day
forth and forevermore. Cake and candle-
blowing privileges included.

Signed: George P. Doon Sr.

With a little bow, Grandfather Doon presented
the document to Felina. "You now have a birthday all
your own," he said. "Next year we will help you cele-
brate it. There'll be cake and ice cream and presents.
Yes siree!"

Felina hugged him tightly. "Oh, Grandfather Doon,
thank you! Thank you and thank you."

Everyone stared at the little witch. It was the very
first time anyone had ever heard her say thank you.
They could tell by her glowing face that she really
meant it.

"There's just one thing more, Felina," said Mrs.
Doon regretfully. "When we do something that hurts
another person we must go and say we're sorry."

"Witches *never* say sorry," Felina retorted instantly.

"I'm afraid you'll have to go down and apologize to
Mrs. Parker and Suzie for spoiling the party," said Mrs.
Doon.

"Let me tell you something, Felina," put in Grandfather Doon, "something I learned when I was just about your age. When you have a difficult duty to perform, there's only one way to lick it. You just stand up tall and do it. Right away, without making a fuss about it. Then it's over in no time.

"If it'll make you feel better," he added, "I'll go along with you to Suzie's house, just for the walk. After all, you own my birthday now, and I feel a wee bit responsible about the owner of that birthday having a good reputation."

"I'll do it," said Felina, "if you'll go with me."

And that's how it was. They went down the street, side by side, and Grandfather Doon stood behind a bush, while Felina went up and knocked at Mrs. Parker's door.

She said, "I'm sorry," very politely, to Mrs. Parker. She said, "I'm sorry," to Suzie, who wasn't crying anymore. Suzie had discovered that the birthday doll, being made of plastic, was washable. It was now as good as new, in spite of having tumbled into the chocolate ice cream.

Suzie and her mother were very nice about it all and accepted Felina's apologies graciously. Mrs. Parker even invited her to "come again." And when Felina went back down the steps her heart felt as light as a baby cloud.

Grandfather held her hand as they returned home. And somebody even said later that they saw *both* Grandfather and Felina skipping, as they went along.

8

Christmas Is Coming!

Thanksgiving Day was cold, crisp, and beautiful. Mrs. Doon stuffed the huge turkey that Grandfather Doon bought. She made two golden pumpkin pies and a great bowl of sparkling red cranberry sauce.

Lucinda and Felina straightened the house and set the table and made place cards for everyone. They colored orange pumpkin faces and put names on them.

They even made one for Itchabody and put it by his dish on the porch. And old Itchabody just stood around waiting and whining hungrily, while the turkey simmered merrily away in the kitchen oven.

Felina ate some of everything. She ate turkey and sweet potatoes and cranberries and pie. She ate until she was stuffed and not once did she mention jibbers' gizzards or black-bat soup.

It was a truly wonderful Turkey Day, and when Grandfather Doon said grace, he added under his breath, "And thank you, dear Lord, for sending us this little witch to love. She certainly makes life interesting. Amen."

When Thanksgiving was over and Itchabody had gobbled the last scrap of leftover turkey, the Doon family began to get ready for Christmas, the biggest day of the year.

Mr. Doon made things in his shop in the garage and kept the door locked. Mrs. Doon made things in the sewing room and warned everyone not to peek. Lucinda and Felina made things at school. They colored Santas and painted Christmas trees on cards.

Soon the house was filled with wonderful smells of fruitcakes baking in the oven. Lucinda and Felina helped cut up fruit and crack nuts. They cut out dozens and dozens of tiny cookies shaped like trees and stars and bells.

Grandfather took them both on his lap and told them the beautiful story of Christmas and the Christ Child.

The whole family went out into the woods and gathered great boughs of evergreens. They gathered red berries to decorate the house. And they made a holly wreath to put on the front door.

Right in the middle of the wreath was a bright red ribbon with a row of silver sleigh bells. It made a lovely jingle-bell sound when friends came to see the family.

Oh, it was an exciting time! And with the happiness and the good food that she ate, Felina's sharp little face began to fill out. She became plump and rosy and looked more and more like a normal little girl and less and less like a witch.

But one day something happened to change everything.

Lucinda had gone up the street for her piano lesson. Miss Gregg, the piano teacher, didn't like Felina to come. She declared that the funny little hat made her so nervous that she skipped a note now and then.

Mrs. Doon was busy in her sewing room. Mr. Doon was down at the newspaper office. And Grandfather Doon had gone to town on a very secret Christmas errand.

So Felina and Itchabody were all alone. They had climbed up in the mulberry tree to think about Christmas.

As they sat there dreaming, Clarence Brown, the big boy who lived next door, chanced to wander through the yard.

Clarence was what is known as a troublemaker. He had pale hair about the color of leftover lemon custard. He had a mean look in his eyes.

The neighbors all hoped that the Brown boy would outgrow his mean streak, but he hadn't done so yet.

It just happened, as he passed under Felina's tree, that an old dry twig fell down. It struck him—just lightly—on the shoulder.

He looked up into the tree and saw Felina and Itchabody. "Oh, it's the little witch," he cried. "What are you doing up there, little witch? Did you throw that stick at me?"

"No," said Felina. She really hadn't. "Itchabody knocked it down." She started to say she was sorry but didn't, because right then Clarence Brown began to say mean things.

"You're a wicked witch," he taunted her. "Came out of the sky on a broom. You won't get anything for Christmas!"

"I will so," said Felina. "All children get something for Christmas."

"That's right," said Clarence, "but witches never do. Didn't you know that? Witches and bad children don't get anything but whips and stones in their socks."

Then he began to sing, in a high, taunting voice:

"A bunch of whips
To make you moan;
A bunch of stones
To break your bones."

"That's not so," sobbed Felina. And she knocked another twig down—accidentally—and it hit him on the top of his lemon-colored head.

"It is so," he shouted. And he said it again, louder. Over and over again. "You're a witch, you're a witch, you're a witch," he added wickedly.

The little witch began to shake. Itchabody was in her arms, and she held him too tight. He began to snarl and scratch.

Then the cat made a sudden scramble and leaped from her arms, down out of the tree. He landed right on the top of Clarence's head.

The boy tore down the street, shrieking at the top of his lungs.

Itchabody didn't hurt Clarence, but he scared him badly. And the little witch screamed after him, "Serves you right, serves you right, serves you right!"

Mrs. Doon heard the screaming and came running out of the house. "What is the matter, Felina?" she asked, looking up into the bare tree. "Come down and I'll give you cookies and milk."

Felina wouldn't move. She just sat there, glaring down. "Don't want any milk," she said. "Don't want any cookies. I'm just a wicked witch, and I won't eat people food."

Mrs. Doon was deeply troubled. She tried for a long time to coax Felina down out of the tree. But Felina wouldn't budge, and she wouldn't say what the trouble was.

When Lucinda came home from her music lesson, she went out into the yard. "Please come down, Felina," she pleaded. "We'll play house. You can have Lucille today, if you like."

But Felina just glared. She wouldn't even answer. She sat there, looking exactly like a horrid little witch.

Not until Mr. Doon came home from work could they do anything with her. He just said, "Get down out of that mulberry tree, Felina—that's an order. If I have to climb up and get you, you'll be sorry."

So Felina came down. But she wouldn't eat any supper. She wouldn't sing Christmas carols around the piano. And she refused to help decorate the Christmas cookies.

"She was getting to be such a sweet little girl," said Mrs. Doon sadly. "I can't understand it."

"Something is worrying her," said Mr. Doon with a frown.

But what it was nobody could even guess. And Felina wouldn't say.

Every day Felina sat in the closet after school. She would talk to no one but Itchabody and she never took off her little cone-shaped hat.

Her small face got thinner and thinner and her nose grew sharper and sharper. And she ate almost nothing at all.

Even Grandfather Doon couldn't make her laugh.

"I'm so worried about her," said Mrs. Doon at last. "I'm sure she's sick. I'm going to take her to see Dr. Perriwinkle."

9

A Visit to Dr. Perriwinkle

The next day Mrs. Doon called Dr. Perriwinkle's office and made an appointment to bring Felina in. The two went to town on the bus to the doctor's office.

Dr. Perriwinkle was a fat little man who looked somewhat like a good-natured squirrel. At first when he saw Felina, he was very jolly. But he soon got over it.

For one thing, every time he bent over to examine Felina's heart with the stethoscope, the point of her peaked witch's hat stuck him in the eye. She wouldn't take it off.

When the nurse tried to weigh her, she jumped up and down so that they couldn't read the scale. The nurse had to write on the record: Weight—Between 49 and 100 pounds.

Dr. Perriwinkle said, "That's no good." And they had to tear up the record and start all over again.

When the doctor asked her to stick out her tongue, she refused. But when he turned his back she stuck it out as far as she could.

Felina didn't want to go to a doctor in the first place. She seemed to be trying to prove just how unco-operative she could be.

"Undernourished," pronounced the doctor at last. "She just isn't getting enough to eat."

"Her appetite is very poor," sighed Mrs. Doon. "I simply can't understand it. She was so well and happy, then all of a sudden she changed."

Dr. Perriwinkle puffed out his cheeks. He looked sternly at Felina. "You'll have to be a good little girl and eat what you're told," he warned, "if you want Santa Claus to bring you anything for Christmas. Santa doesn't like naughty children, you know."

"Santa's a silly old fool," said Felina crossly. Then she looked a bit frightened. "And I'm *not* a little girl. I'm a bad witch," she told him.

"Oh, dear," said Mrs. Doon. She began to put Felina's dress back on.

"I'll give you a tonic for her," said Dr. Perriwinkle.

He looked pretty exhausted by this time. "What she really needs," he added as he wrote out the prescrip-tion, "is glub, glubble, glubble."

It sounded very much like he had said, "A good spanking." But Mrs. Doon wasn't sure.

Felina made another face at him.

Almost as soon as poor Mrs. Doon got the little witch home again and sent her upstairs to change her dress, the phone rang. It was Dr. Perriwinkle calling.

He spluttered so much as he talked that it was hard to understand him. But Mrs. Doon thought that he said something about losing his stepladder.

"Your what?" asked Mrs. Doon.

"My *stethoscope*," he yelled into her ear. "That child of yours—that little witch—it was right here around my neck when she was in the office. When my next patient came in, it was gone."

"Oh, I'm sure Felina wouldn't—" said Mrs. Doon weakly. But of course she wasn't sure at all, and as soon as she had hung up the phone she went straight upstairs.

There, in the corner of the closet, was Felina. She was listening to Itchabody's heart go blub-a, blub-a, blub-a—with Dr. Perriwinkle's stethoscope.

Dangling from under Felina's peaked black hat was more of the good doctor's equipment. Adhesive tape and gauze, and a thermometer.

"Oh, Felina," said Mrs. Doon wearily. "Whatever are we going to do about you."

Then, busy as she was, she had to take Felina and the stethoscope back uptown to the doctor's office. And Felina was made to say, "I'm sorry," which she did. But not very prettily.

And the doctor looked as though he didn't want an apology. All he wanted was his stethoscope back and a little rest. Just before they left the office, he recommended another doctor for Felina.

"After all," he said, when the door had closed behind his strange patient, "I'm a people doctor, not a witch doctor!"

10

In a Witch's Sock

Mr. Doon had to order Felina to take the tonic that Dr. Perriwinkle had prescribed.

"Tastes like the old Wizard's poison brew," she insisted, making a terrible face every time. "He makes it out of mustard seeds and polliwog tails. It's sure to kill me."

The tonic didn't seem to do much good. Felina continued to be a very miserable little witch. She took no interest in the Christmas preparations. She refused to play with Lucinda.

No matter how hard people tried to be nice to her, she tried just as hard to be wicked. Wherever she went people would ask her if she had been good all year. And somebody always said, "Santa knows. He brings toys only to good little boys and girls."

And whenever the little witch was in a bad mood, her Small Magic got to working again. One day Mr. Doon found all of his good ties mysteriously tied into knots. And Mrs. Doon discovered that the Christmas candles that she had on the mantel wouldn't stay lit.

Worst of all, Lucinda's favorite princess doll, Lucille, was missing. They looked under the bed and in the closet. They couldn't find Lucille anywhere.

"Did *you* take her, Felina?" demanded Lucinda crossly. "I believe you did."

It wasn't at all like Lucinda to be cross with the little witch, for she loved Felina. But she loved her doll, too.

Felina simply wouldn't answer. She spent most of her time in the closet, whispering witch charms into Itchabody's small pointed ears.

The Doons were very patient with Felina. They knew that something must be very, very wrong. And Mr. Doon was seldom heard to say *that's an order*, unless it was absolutely necessary.

At last, it was the night before Christmas.

"Come, Felina," said Lucinda. "Let's hang our socks by the chimney."

"Not me," said Felina. "I won't get anything for Christmas. I know I won't, 'cause I'm a witch. I just want to go back up there." She pointed toward the sky from which she had fallen when she broke her broom.

So Lucinda hung up her sock all by herself. She felt very sad. And when Grandfather Doon read *The Night Before Christmas* to them, Lucinda didn't smile once.

Felina stubbornly put her hands over her ears. But

not very tightly, for her eyes kept getting bigger and bigger as the story of Santa unfolded. She was very quiet when she crept up to bed in her pajamas.

In the middle of the night Mr. Doon thought he heard a strange sound on the stairs.

He opened his bedroom door a crack and looked out. He saw a thin little figure in a black pointed hat creeping down the stairs. She had a sock in her hand, and she found her way through the dark. She hung the sock on the nail that Mr. Doon had put for her by the fireplace.

When he went later to tuck the children in, Felina was sound asleep. This time, when Mr. Doon bent to kiss his own sleeping daughter, he also kissed Felina, very tenderly, on the cheek.

"Poor mixed-up little witch," he said.

On Christmas morning, bright and early, Lucinda reached over and pulled Felina's shiny black pigtail.

"Merry Christmas! Merry Christmas!" she cried. "Wake up, sleepyhead. Let's go down and see what we have under the tree."

Felina pretended to be sound asleep. After Lucinda had put on slippers and robe and gone downstairs, Felina followed. Very slowly. Her green eyes were big and anxious in her little face.

"Oh, look, look!" cried Lucinda.

From the middle of the stairs, Felina could see it all.

In one corner was a big Christmas tree, lighted with a hundred lights and glowing with beautiful colored ornaments. On the very tip-top was a white-clad angel with spreading wings.

Under the tree—oh, under the tree there were wonderful things to see. Toys and books and packages still to be opened.

Right in the middle of it all sat two lovely dolls. One was a bride doll, which Lucinda had been asking for. But the other—the other was the strangest dolly you ever saw. She wore a long black robe and a tiny pointed witch's hat.

She had a tiny broom under her arm. And it wasn't broken.

Felina came slowly down the steps. She didn't know it, but right behind her came Mr. Doon and Mrs. Doon and Grandfather Doon. All in robes and slippers—all waiting to see what would happen.

"Look, look, Felina," cried Lucinda. "I told you you'd get presents for Christmas." And she ran to Felina with the witch doll and put it in her arms.

"For me?" said Felina. "Really for me?"

She held the doll close to her heart and turned her questioning face to Mrs. Doon, who now stood right beside her.

"I dressed it for you, Felina. Just for you," said Mrs. Doon. "Now why don't you look in your sock, to see what Santa brought you?"

Felina clung tightly to the witch doll and walked hesitantly to the bulging sock near the fireplace. She sat down and dumped the contents into her lap.

There was a big round orange, nuts and candy, a red-and-white cane—and a big shiny silver dollar in the toe!

Felina looked up. There was wonder in her small face and her eyes were like a couple of jewels. "But where," she asked, "where are the whips and stones?"

"Whips and stones, darling?" Mrs. Doon frowned. "I don't understand."

"I thought that was what bad girls and witches got from Santa," said Felina. "That's what Clarence Brown told me. He said:

> "'A bunch of whips
> To make you moan;
> A bunch of stones
> To break your bones.'"

Mrs. Doon knelt down and hugged the little girl and kissed her cheek.

"But you *aren't* a bad little girl, Felina," she said. "You're our dear, dear little witch, and I don't know what we'd ever do without you."

That's when Mr. Doon was heard to say through his teeth, "I know what I'd like to do. I'd like to give that Clarence Brown a *sock full of rocks to knock off his block!*"

"Now, George," scolded Mrs. Doon gently, "remember, it is Christmas."

"I'm sorry," said Mr. Doon. But he didn't look too sorry.

Then Grandfather shouted, "A merry, merry Christmas, everybody!" He began to laugh his wonderful laugh and to pass out presents all around.

There were shiny skis, a red sled—and a record player for Mother. There was even a new red collar with a tiny bell on it for Itchabody.

It was a beautiful Christmas. And the surprises weren't over. Felina and Lucinda flew happily upstairs again to bring down all the presents they had made at school.

There were flowerpots for Mother, made from old coffee cans, nicely painted. There were pottery ashtrays for Mr. Doon. And a scrapbook full of jolly snapshots for Grandfather Doon to take home to New Haven.

That night, very mysteriously, Lucinda's doll, Lucille, materialized once more in her cradle. She had been hiding in the mulberry tree all the time, and it was strange that nobody had thought to look for her there.

11

The Snow Witch

On New Year's Eve, Mr. Doon awoke the children from a sound sleep, at exactly one minute to midnight. He had promised them that they could help ring in the New Year.

At first they could hardly hold their eyes open. But the noise soon brought them to their senses.

Bells were clanging. Firecrackers were banging. Horns were blowing. All down the block on Mockingbird Lane people were shouting "Happy New Year" to one another and singing "Auld Lang Syne."

Grandfather went to the kitchen and got tin pans and big spoons.

"Happy New Year!" he shouted, as everybody in the family banged merrily away on a tin pan. "Happy, happy New Year."

It was exciting and fun. And when all the noise died down, Mr. Doon opened the door, and they stood looking outside.

Snow was falling in great white flakes. Falling. Falling. The ground was all glistening and white where the light lay upon it.

"It's beautiful," said Felina, in wonder. "It sounds like silence." And it did. For the snow fell so softly— shhh, shhh, shhh.

"It *is* beautiful," said Mrs. Doon seriously. "A new year, and three hundred and sixty-five clean new pages for us to write our lives on. I hope the pages will be full of happiness for this family."

And she put her arms about the two little girls and shooed them back up to bed.

In the morning Felina and Lucinda begged to go out in the wonderful snow to play. So Mrs. Doon bundled them up in red snowsuits.

Lucinda wore a red hood, but Felina clung to her little witch's hat. Mrs. Doon tied a warm scarf under it, so her ears wouldn't get nipped.

"I do wish she'd let me throw away that awful hat," said Mrs. Doon, as she and her husband watched the two little figures clown in the snow.

"I don't think it will be long now," said George Doon thoughtfully.

And he was right.

When the neighborhood children saw Lucinda and Felina tumbling in the snowbanks and throwing big, soft balls at each other, they all came running to join in the fun.

"Let's make a snowman," cried one of the little boys.

"Oh, let's!" shouted Lucinda.

So they all pitched in to help. Scooping up the feathery white snow in their mittens, they shaped and patted the snow in a mound, making it higher and higher.

A body, a head, two arms—soon it looked like a big white-clad person. They used two pieces of coal for eyes. Someone patted on a pointed nose. And someone ran home and brought back an old broom to put under the snowman's arm.

Then one of the children shouted, "Oh, see—the broom, the pointed nose. It looks like a witch—or a wizard!"

And so it did. The face had a sharp, wicked look—just like a wizard's.

"Now all we need is a hat," declared another child. "We need a peaked witch's hat."

Everyone looked right at Felina. At the funny little black hat, perched on her woolly scarf.

She backed away, staring at the children and hanging on to her hat with two mittened hands.

"Oh, lend us your hat, Felina," they cried.

"Yes, do," pleaded Lucinda. Her blue eyes were sparkling with fun as she looked into Felina's little face. "Give us your hat. You aren't a witch anymore—you don't need it."

They weren't making fun of her. They were laughing and gay, their faces full of friendliness.

And all at once, Felina grabbed off the hat and held it out to the clamoring children. She wanted to give up the funny hat. She wanted to give it to the snow witch.

So the tallest boy climbed on a box and put the hat on the snow witch's head. It added the perfect touch.

All the children danced around and around the strange white figure, laughing and chanting. And Felina laughed with them.

She had never been happier in her life.

And when Mrs. Doon looked out of the window and saw the familiar little hat on the snowman, she laughed softly too.

"We've lost our little witch," said Grandfather Doon somewhat wistfully.

It was true. Nobody ever thought of calling Felina a witch again. Not even Clarence Brown, who had probably learned *his* lesson when Itchabody landed on his head.

At first Felina seemed a little nervous without her hat. She kept reaching up and touching her head to see if it was there. For three days the snow witch stood in the yard, wearing the hat. Then one morning, when the children went out to play, there was no hat on the snow witch. The hat had disappeared.

Someone swore it had been seen flying through the sky by itself. But Felina said, "The old Wizard reached down through the wind with his broom and swept it away."

She didn't seem to mind at all. After the holidays were over and Grandfather Doon had flown in the jet plane back to New Haven, Felina went back to school wearing a woolly hood, just like the other little girls.

With her pretty shining hair and her plump rosy face, she looked so much like an ordinary human child, no one would ever have suspected she had been a witch.

One day, in the spring, when the snow had melted from the ground, Felina found the bedraggled little hat against the back fence. It had been lost in the snow. She brought it into the house.

"See what I found," she said to Mrs. Doon. "It looks like a witch's hat."

"So it does," said Mrs. Doon. She looked into Felina's big green eyes. "Do you want me to clean it for you, Felina?" she asked.

Felina laughed. "Why, it's an old witch's hat," she replied. "What would I want with a witch's hat?"

So the hat was finally thrown away. When Mrs. Doon took the girls shopping that spring, to buy material for Easter dresses, Felina said, "Please, may my dolly have a new Easter outfit too? I don't want a witch doll anymore. I want a princess doll."

So the little witch doll was turned into a princess

too. And only Itchabody cried when the tiny pointed cap and black dress were packed away high on the shelf.

"Meoooooow!" he whined.

He must have known that that was the end of the little witch.

12

Halloween and Happy Birthday

It seems a little sad, but perhaps it is a good thing—
when Felina lost her witch's hat, she also lost her magic.
Her bad magic, that is.

She went to school like all normal little girls. She
learned many things. She learned to read well, and to
write, and she started to pick out tunes on the piano.
So Mr. Doon had her take piano lessons, along with
Lucinda.

Miss Gregg didn't mind having Felina come, now
that she wasn't wearing the "eerie" witch's hat. In fact,
she thought Felina was quite talented, and said she
had "magic" in her fingers, which was really quite a
joke.

Now, Felina didn't change into a perfect little angel.
She still got into mischief once in a while. Sometimes
she was cross, and sometimes she refused to eat her
spinach. But usually she was a very dear little girl, and
the Doon family loved her more and more.

They took her everywhere they went. On picnics
and to the zoo, to the museums and to the movies. The

happy days sped by. The weeks sped by. The months sped by.

A whole year passed. It was Halloween once more. And Halloween was a very special day for Felina. For *two* reasons, you may remember. First, it was the anniversary of the time when the little witch appeared at Lucinda's window.

And second—it was her birthday!

Mrs. Doon planned a surprise party for Felina. And Grandfather Doon flew out from New Haven early that year, so he would be there for the occasion. After all, it *had* been his birthday, and he thought that he did deserve a piece of cake.

All of the children in the neighborhood were invited. They came in costume. There were ghosts and goblins and clowns and pirates.

Lucinda was a pirate with a patch over one eye. Felina was a clown in a polka-dot suit and a white mask.

They had pumpkins and balloons and played Pin the Rib on the Skeleton. Mr. Doon did magic tricks out of a book and made everyone laugh.

Then Grandfather Doon popped in, dressed like a huge gray spook, carrying a basket of birthday gifts for Felina. And just then Mrs. Doon came from the kitchen with a big cake with white icing and orange-colored candles. There were eight candles—and one to grow on.

"Happy birthday, Felina," sang everyone. "Happy birthday, dear Felina."

Felina's eyes gleamed through her mask as she puffed out the candles and made her wish.

She didn't tell a soul what her wish was, of course, because that would have spoiled the spell. But on the very last page of this book it may come true.

Then Grandfather Doon lifted up his spook mask and demanded his piece of cake. Felina laughed and gave him the biggest piece of all.

After the party, all of the children—that is, all of the ghosts and goblins and clowns and pirates— went around the neighborhood, playing Trick or Treat.

As Felina and Lucinda ran up the block, Mr. Doon stood on the porch, with a smile on his face.

Suddenly, a big gust of wind blew out of the sky. A mysterious black cloud crossed over the moon. Looking up, Mr. Doon was quite sure he saw an old witch riding through the sky on her broom.

"Come, Felina," a voice in the wind seemed to be saying. "Come, little witch, and jump on my broom. Come, come, little witch."

Mr. Doon shook his fist at the black-clad figure. "No witch lives in this house, old woman," he said. "Just two little girls."

The moaning voice died out of the sky.

The next day Mr. Doon came home early from the newspaper office.

"We have an appointment with the judge," he said to the family. "We have to renew our permit to keep Felina—if we want her to be our little girl, that is."

"Oh, we do," cried Lucinda.

So all of the Doons, including Grandfather, put on their very best clothes and polished their shoes and went to the courthouse.

The same old judge looked down from his bench and stared at Felina.

Her hair was smoothly combed and she was standing very politely, looking up at him.

"Ahem," said the old judge, "this can't be the same little witch who stood before me last year."

"No, your honor," said Mr. Doon. "That was a little lost witch, but this is a little girl. We have learned to love her very dearly and we want to adopt her."

"Well, well," said the judge, peering through his bifocal glasses at his papers. "It seems nobody has claimed her, and it is not likely that anyone is going to. I suppose you want a permanent permit this time."

"Indeed we do," said Mrs. Doon.

The judge began to write on a form. "And how old are you, little girl?" he asked.

"I'm eight years old," said Felina. "And my birthday

is October thirty-first. And it's really mine, because my Grandfather Doon gave it to me."

"I certainly did," said Grandfather Doon. "Signed, sealed, and delivered, that's what it is." He took Felina's hand in his and held it tightly.

"And what is your name?" asked the judge.

"My name is Felina," the little girl said politely. "But oh, please, sir," she added, "may I change it? I do like cats, but I don't want to be named after one."

"Well, what do you want to be called?"

"May I please be named Mary—?"

"Why, that's *my* name," said Mrs. Doon, very much pleased.

"Lucinda—" went on Felina.

"And that's *my* name," cried that little girl happily.

"George," added Felina firmly.

"And that's *my* name," said Mr. Doon in surprise.

"Very well," said the judge. "That will be your new name." He wrote it carefully on the form in front of him. "Mary Lucinda George—permanently adopted by the Doon family."

He signed the paper with a flourish and handed it to Mr. Doon. "There will be no charge this time," he remarked.

"Thank you, your honor," said George Doon. "Thank you very much."

Then Grandfather was rounding them all up and

pushing them toward the door. "This is a great day for the Doons," he declared. "It calls for a real celebration. We'll go to the restaurant and have the finest dinner in town."

As the proud little family left the courtroom, the old judge took one last curious look at Felina—oh, no—at Mary Lucinda George, the wicked little witch who had been changed into a happy child.

He shook his gray head in wonder. "It must be magic," he muttered. "Pure magic."

ABOUT THE AUTHOR

Florence Laughlin is the author of several books for children, including *The Seventh Cousin*.

DID YOU
LOVE THIS BOOK?

Simon & Schuster

IN THE bookloop

Join *In the Book Loop* on Everloop.
Find more book lovers online and
read for FREE!

Log on to everloop.com
to join now!

everloop™
Our site. Our stuff. Our world.
www.everloop.com

No Chickens
Allowed.

Real girls just like you from Courtney Sheinmel

PRINT AND EBOOK EDITIONS AVAILABLE
From Simon & Schuster Books for Young Readers
KIDS.SimonandSchuster.com

Join Megan, Cassidy, Emma, and Jess as they experience the ups and downs of middle school along with their favorite classic literary characters!

Drama is required reading.
THE Mother-DAUGHTER BOOK CLUB
HEATHER VOGEL FREDERICK

The Mother-Daughter Book Club
MUCH Ado ABOUT Anne
HEATHER VOGEL FREDERICK

The Mother-Daughter Book Club
DEAR PEN PAL
HEATHER VOGEL FREDERICK

The Mother-Daughter Book Club
PIES & PREJUDICE
HEATHER VOGEL FREDERICK

EBOOK EDITIONS ALSO AVAILABLE
From Simon & Schuster Books for Young Readers
KIDS.SimonandSchuster.com